NEPTUNE ADVENTURES

#5 HURRICANE RESCUE

Other
NEPTUNE ADVENTURES
by Susan Saunders
from Avon Camelot

(#1) DANGER ON CRAB ISLAND
(#2) DISASTER AT PARSONS POINT
(#3) THE DOLPHIN TRAP
(#4) STRANDING ON CEDAR POINT

Coming Soon

(#6) RED TIDE ALERT

Avon Books are available at special quantity discounts for bulk purchases for sales promotions, premiums, fund raising or educational use. Special books, or book excerpts, can also be created to fit specific needs.

For details write or telephone the office of the Director of Special Markets, Avon Books, Inc., Dept. FP, 1350 Avenue of the Americas, New York, New York 10019, 1-800-238-0658.

#5 HURRICANE RESCUE

SUSAN SAUNDERS

AN AVON CAMELOT BOOK

To Dr. Morris W. Greenberg

This is a work of fiction. Names, characters, places, and incidents either are the product of the author's imagination or are used fictitiously. Any resemblance to actual events, locales, organizations, or persons, living or dead, is entirely coincidental and beyond the intent of either the author or the publisher.

AVON BOOKS, INC.
1350 Avenue of the Americas
New York, New York 10019

Copyright © 1998 by Susan Saunders
Published by arrangement with the author
Visit our website at http://www.AvonBooks.com
Library of Congress Catalog Card Number: 98-92790
ISBN: 0-380-80252-X

All rights reserved, which includes the right to reproduce this book or portions thereof in any form whatsoever except as provided by the U.S. Copyright Law. For information address Avon Books, Inc.

First Avon Camelot Printing: October 1998

CAMELOT TRADEMARK REG. U.S. PAT. OFF. AND IN OTHER COUNTRIES, MARCA REGISTRADA, HECHO EN U.S.A.

Printed in the U.S.A.

OPM 10 9 8 7 6 5 4 3 2 1

> If you purchased this book without a cover, you should be aware that this book is stolen property. It was reported as "unsold and destroyed" to the publisher, and neither the author nor the publisher has received any payment for this "stripped book."

CHAPTER ONE

"Is Jake hiding in here?" Dana Chapin asked, peering into her cousin Tyler's room. Jake was Dana's big yellow Lab, and he usually hung out with her or with Tyler when they were at home.

Tyler shook his head, and Dana went on, "As soon as anyone starts packing, he disappears, afraid he's about to be banished to Willow Creek Kennels."

Tyler stuffed one last T-shirt into his duffel and zipped it closed. "Nothing for Jake to worry about this time," he said. "He'll be kicking back in comfort at Kim's house."

Kim Meyers was Dana's best friend, and Dana and Jake would be staying with her while Mr. and Mrs. Chapin attended a stranding conference on the West Coast. Tyler was going to spend all four days with Charlie and Carter, the Mote twins.

And school's starting at the end of next week. . . . I can't believe summer's almost over! Dana said to herself.

"What about behind the couch in the living room?" Tyler suggested. "Jake can squeeze himself into some pretty skinny spaces."

"No, he's not there," Dana said. "Hey—maybe he's in the basement."

"I'm finished, so I'll help you look for him," Tyler said.

The cousins headed down the hall, stopping to glance under Dana's bed again, then checking her parents' room, too. Dana's mom was standing beside the rolltop desk, digging through a red canvas carryall.

"Are you two ready?" Mrs. Chapin asked them, then continued under her breath, "laptop, recorder, notebooks, plane tickets . . ."

"Jake?" Dana added to her list.

"He's outside with your dad," her mom said. "We're keeping an eye on him until it's time to leave." She looked at her watch. "And I think we'd better start loading the truck. A half hour or so to drop you two and Jake off in Rockport, then an hour's drive to the airport in Wilton. . . ."

"We'll get Dad," Dana said.

She and Tyler dumped their duffels near the kitchen door and ran down the back steps.

Dana had lived in the two-hundred-year-old lighthouse at Parsons Point all of her life. Her parents had bought the place thirteen years ago, when they started Project Neptune, an organization that rescues sick and injured sea animals and nurses them back to health.

Dana had been dealing with recuperating seals, dolphins, and sea turtles since she was big enough to carry a food bucket. Her cousin Tyler had only been at the Point since January, but he'd caught on fast to the routine.

"Hang on—I want to check out Bonnie and Claude," Tyler said to Dana as they hurried toward the large stranding barn on the far side of the gravel road.

Bonnie and Claude were two of the latest arrivals at the Point. A pair of young pilot whales, they'd washed up on a beach not far from Rockport, along with many members of their pod. Several of the adult whales had died there or were in such poor shape that they had had to be put to sleep by Dr. Martin Bucalo, Project Neptune's veterinarian. But Claude and Bonnie were well enough, and small enough, to be moved by boat to Parsons Point and into the outdoor dolphin pool.

At first the little whales had lain at the bottom of the pool, barely moving. They'd refused to eat and were in danger of dying from thirst, since pilot whales got all their water from the fish they swallowed. Several Project Neptune volunteers had joined Bonnie and Claude in the dolphin pool, pried the whales' mouths open, and forced down herring and squid stuffed with vitamins and medicine. Soon Bonnie and Claude had started eating on their own.

Now the pilot whales were recovering their strength. They scuffled over the fish thrown to them at feeding time. They chased each other around the pool and played hide-and-seek with their human visitors. That morning, Claude poked his head out of the water to watch Dana and Tyler walking toward him. Dana knew it was Claude because of the wavy notch in the leading edge of his dorsal fin.

A couple of seconds later, Bonnie popped up, too. She was the smaller of the two, around eight and a half feet long. Claude was closer to ten feet, and he weighed about a thousand pounds. The young whales looked a lot like dolphins, only much larger, with bulging foreheads and taller dorsal fins. They were darker than dolphins, too, with black backs and gray stomachs.

Bonnie and Claude gazed at the Chapins for a moment. They whistled loudly a couple of times. Then they sank slowly out of sight. They leaped out of the water on the far side of the pool, only to smack down flat on the surface, sending a fountain of spray into the air. They jackknifed and swam in a circle upside down near the bottom.

"I can't believe how much energy they have—week before last, they were nearly dead," Tyler said to Dana in a low voice.

It was a rule at the Point never to talk directly to the recovering animals. If something had to be said within earshot of them, volunteers always tried to whisper. The motto of Project Neptune was "heal and release," and the less contact the animals had with human beings, the easier it would be for them to adjust to life in the wild again.

Now Claude and Bonnie were streaking from one side

of the pool to the other, playing follow-the-leader, their broad black fins leaving V-shaped wakes on top of the water.

"Mom thinks we probably won't have to keep them here past the end of November," Dana whispered.

"They should be plenty strong enough to manage on their own by then. Plus they'll be getting too big for this pool. Hey, there's Uncle Joe," Tyler added, pointing toward the back of the stranding barn.

Dana's dad was pounding nails into the siding, close to one of the old copper downspouts.

"And Jake," said Dana. Her dog was dozing in the sun near Mr. Chapin's toolbox. "Let's grab him."

"Dad, Mom says it's time to start loading the truck," Dana said when she and Tyler were close enough. "Reach for Jake's collar," she murmured under her breath to her cousin. The dog was already scrambling to his feet, peering around for an escape route.

"I'm almost done here," Mr. Chapin said. He drove a nail into the bracket that held the downspout tight against the side of the barn. "I want to make sure there's nothing that can blow loose, just in case that storm tracks up the coast," he added.

"What storm?" Dana said.

"Hurricane Fiona," said her dad.

"But I thought it was supposed to make landfall in Virginia or Maryland," Dana said. "That's what the weather guys are predicting."

"No one really knows what a storm will do," Mr. Chapin said, pounding in another nail.

"Wow—a hurricane at Parsons Point?" said Tyler excitedly. He and his dad, Dana's uncle Jim, lived in Fairbanks, Alaska, where hurricanes just didn't happen.

Even Parsons Point was far enough up the Atlantic coast to be out of range of most tropical storms. There had only been two hurricanes that Dana could remember herself: Hurricane Patricia had swung inland about a hundred miles below Rockport, the July that Dana was seven. And Hurricane Eric had traveled up the East Coast the September that she'd started fifth grade. By the time the storms had reached the Point, neither had been any more powerful than a strong winter nor'easter.

But Dana had heard plenty of stories about the famous hurricane of 1958, Hurricane Maxine. Several Neptuners—that's what the Project Neptune volunteers called themselves—had lived through it. Mr. Garber, the oldest Neptuner, had lost part of his house to the wind, which had gusted at over 170 miles per hour.

But even more dangerous than the wind was the storm surge. Hurricane Maxine had piled the ocean water into a giant wave that had swept over Crab Island and across Badger Bay into the town of Rockport. It had destroyed everything in its path and left three feet of mud behind on Main Street. Ten people had drowned, and many houses and downtown businesses had washed away with hardly a trace.

Thinking about that giant wave always gave Dana a

chill, and she had to remind herself that Parsons Point had weathered the hurricane of '58 safely, and lots more storms besides.

The lighthouse has been standing for two hundred years. It's not going anywhere for at least two hundred more, Dana said to herself. *And the Point will be here forever.*

Parsons Point rose seventy feet above the Atlantic, and it wasn't made of shifting sand, either. It was formed of solid granite bedrock, the same stone that the builders had used for the tower of the lighthouse two centuries earlier.

Still . . . Dana stared suspiciously across the cliffs, out at the blue-green Atlantic. The day was calm, and the surface of the ocean was as flat as a lake. There weren't even any clouds in the sky.

"Don't wish for a hurricane, Tyler," Dana's dad was saying. "*We* can always evacuate before a storm hits, move inland until it's over. But we can't do anything about the animals in the stranding barn. Where could we board twelve or fourteen wild seals and a couple of sea turtles?"

"And two pilot whales," Dana added.

"You're right," said Tyler. But he glanced at the sky, too, probably scouting for promising storm clouds.

Mr. Chapin dropped his hammer into the toolbox. "If it weren't for the talk we're scheduled to give about the oil spill off Gull Island, we'd cancel our trip and stick around, just in case," he said to Dana and Tyler. "But maybe everyone will luck out, and Hurricane Fiona will make a sharp right turn and drift farther out to sea, where she won't bother anybody. Are you two packed?" he asked them.

"Ready to go," Tyler said, with a firm grip on Jake's collar.

"So am I," said Dana.

"It'll only take a few minutes to load the truck. We'll be in Rockport by . . . two-thirty," Mr. Chapin said, checking his watch.

Parsons Point poked out of the mainland like an index finger, its tip and south side facing into the Atlantic and its north side edging Badger Bay. The town of Rockport was straight across the bay, about five miles from the lighthouse at the end of Harbor Lane.

By 2:35, Dana and Jake were climbing out of the truck in front of the Meyerses' house on Lilac Place in Rockport. Kim ran down her front walk to meet them.

"Hi, Mr. Chapin, Mrs. Chapin. Hey, Tyler," Kim said, adding, "Mom and Dad are at work, but they're coming home early." Mr. and Mrs. Meyers ran WLIR, the small Rockport television station.

Kim opened the truck door for Dana. "Let me carry your duffel."

"I'll take Jake's stuff," Dana said, climbing out, "and Jake." She held on to the end of the dog's leather leash while her dad set a shopping bag full of dry dog food and dog toys down beside them.

Mr. Chapin lifted Dana's bike from the back of the truck

and steered it onto the Meyerses' sidewalk. "We'd better hurry," he said, kissing Dana on top of her head. "Have a good time, and we'll pick you up Sunday evening."

"If you need to talk to us about anything at all, you have our number at the hotel in San Diego," said her mom, hugging Dana through the truck window.

"I have it in my backpack," Dana said.

"And we'll be calling you every day," said Mrs. Chapin.

"Maybe I'll see you later this afternoon," Tyler told Dana from the backseat.

"Come on, Jakie," Kim said, taking the dog's leash from Dana.

"Give a good speech, and have fun!" Dana said to her parents as her dad climbed back into the driver's seat.

Dana, Kim, and Jake watched the truck rolling up Lilac Place. The dog whined and fidgeted a little. Then, the instant the truck turned the corner onto Briermere, Jake lunged forward. He pulled Kim down onto one knee and almost jerked his leash out of her hand.

"Jake, where do you think you're going?" Dana said sharply, grabbing hold of the leash, too. *"No!"*

"Wow—he is *strong*," Kim said, standing up again. "What's the problem, Jake?" she asked the dog.

"He was trying to follow the truck," Dana said.

"Let's put him in the backyard," Kim said, starting up the walk with Jake, "before he's halfway to Wilton."

CHAPTER TWO

Charlie and Carter Mote were Tyler's best friends at Rockport Middle School, and they'd asked him to stay at their house while Uncle Joe and Aunt Lissa were away. The Motes were the first friends Tyler had made here, right after he'd come to the Point from Alaska last January. He hadn't really known anyone, not even his cousin. He and Dana had only met a couple of times before in their entire lives, and—besides the same last name—they didn't have much in common.

Tyler had been seriously lonely. He'd been homesick for his dad, and for his Malamute, Thane. He'd missed his friends back in Fairbanks, too. He'd wondered how he was ever going to get through the next twelve months, which was how long his dad would be living in the Canadian Arctic, studying a wolf pack.

Then Tyler had noticed Carter Mote in his seventh-grade math class. Actually, he'd noticed what Carter was doing, which was drawing amazing pictures of superheroes and spaceships and monsters in a red spiral notebook.

"Very cool!" Tyler had whispered.

Carter had just smiled—he never talked much. But when class was over, Tyler had met Charlie Mote out in the hall, and Charlie always talked enough for both of them.

The Motes were twins—not identical, but very similar: tall, bony, and blond. And they had their own way of dressing. They took turns wearing their dad's huge old Army jacket, their black high-tops had holes in the toes, and they owned an assortment of ancient flannel shirts that looked a lot like pajama tops. Sometimes the twins even cut their own hair.

Aunt Lissa said the Mote boys dressed the way they did because there weren't any grown-ups around to supervise. Their mother didn't live with them, and their dad worked a lot of the time. He was a commercial fisherman with his own boat, the *Bonnie Jean*.

There was no mom in Tyler's house in Fairbanks, either. Tyler's mom had died when Tyler was a baby. And he was on his own some of the time when his dad was working. Jim Chapin was a biologist like Joe and Lissa, his brother and sister-in-law. So Tyler sort of understood how the twins lived. Plus he liked their style, although lots of the Rockport kids didn't. Even Dana had always thought the Motes were too weird to hang around with. But now that she was getting to know them a little better because of Tyler, she was starting to think they were okay, too.

Uncle Joe turned another corner, onto Roanoke Avenue, and Tyler leaned forward. "There it is," he said, pointing down the street. "The blue house with the crooked chimney."

"Oh, dear—I've never really taken a hard look at it before," Aunt Lissa murmured, staring through the windshield as they rolled closer to the house.

"Tyler, are you sure you wouldn't rather stay with the Bucalos?" she asked him. "You and Luke could go kayaking." Luke was Dr. Bucalo's son.

"I'll be fine, Aunt Lissa," Tyler said. "And you've already spoken to Mr. Mote," he added. "They're expecting me."

But he admitted to himself that the Motes' house *was* a little run-down on the outside. Blue paint had flaked off in several places, exposing dark-gray boards underneath. The leaning chimney had lost some bricks. A downstairs window had a cracked pane. The screen door was torn near the bottom.

And Tyler had never been inside—what could that be like? He wasn't sure whether the twins hadn't asked him to stay over before because they were embarrassed about their house or if it was because of Mr. Mote's feelings about the Chapins and Project Neptune. The Motes' dad had no patience with an organization that saved seals and dolphins, since he thought sea mammals were nuisances that ate too many fish.

He was coming around a little, though. Mr. Mote had helped out when there'd been an oil spill off Gull Island, bringing injured animals to the stranding barn at the Point. He'd even invited Tyler and Dana onto the *Bonnie Jean* during the Maritime Festival.

As their truck stopped beside the front gate, Uncle Joe wondered aloud, "How many cats?"

"Uh . . . eight or ten?" Tyler guessed, glancing around the yard. He counted three gray ones, two with black-and-white patches, a couple of reds, and a solid black one.

Then the twins called out from the far side of the house where they were standing beside what looked like a kid's wading pool.

"There's Charlie. And Carter," Tyler said, picking up his duffel.

"Tyler, you're certain there'll be an adult around?" Aunt Lissa said, opening her door. "I don't see any cars in the driveway. . . ."

"Charlie and Carter's granddad will be here all four days—Mr. Mote promised you, right?" Tyler said, sliding out of the truck. "You guys had better get moving, or you'll miss your plane."

"Okay—you have our phone number," his uncle said, lifting out Tyler's bike.

"You'll call the Bucalos to come for you if you have any problems," Aunt Lissa added.

"I won't have any, Aunt Lissa. Don't worry," Tyler

said, shouldering his duffel and grabbing the handlebars of his bike.

He thought his aunt definitely looked worried, though, staring back anxiously at the house as she and his uncle drove away.

"Hey, Tyler!" Carter said, waving him over.

"Drop your duffel on the porch and come meet Grandpa Mote," said Charlie.

Tyler tossed his duffel onto the front steps, leaned his bike against the house, and joined them. The twins were both holding white plastic buckets.

"What are those for?" Tyler asked.

"Minnows," Carter said, showing Tyler a few dozen small, silvery fish in his bucket.

"Our granddad brought over a tubful of 'em to use for bait while he's here. He's in the tackle shed," Charlie said.

They led Tyler around the house, water sloshing in the buckets and a parade of cats trailing along. "Grandpa's taking us fishing," Charlie explained.

A small man in overalls walked out of a wooden shed in the Motes' backyard. He had thinning white hair, an amazingly long, white, wispy beard that reached to the center of his chest, and bright green eyes.

"Grandpa, this is Tyler," Charlie said.

"Our best friend," Carter added.

Grandpa Mote didn't speak—he just nodded, which Tyler was used to because of Carter. He also stuck out his hand.

"Nice to meet you," Tyler said, shaking hands.

For a little old guy, Grandpa Mote had a surprisingly strong grip.

"Poles," the twins' grandfather said, stepping into the shed again.

There was all kinds of cool stuff hanging from the walls and ceiling of the shed or piled in the corners: fishing rods of different lengths, scoop nets, gaffs, a clamming rake and wire basket, some lobster pots, even some handmade wooden floats with MOTE scratched into them.

"Grandpa made those floats when he was eighteen," Charlie said when he noticed Tyler looking at them. "He's seventy-six now."

Tyler glanced at the twins' grandfather. Grandpa Mote was so wrinkled and weathered from years of working outdoors that he could have been ninety. But he hadn't slowed down any. He quickly chose six-foot fishing rods for each of the boys and took a longer one for himself.

"Got those minnows?" he said to Charlie and Carter, sticking a finger into each of the buckets and stirring around.

"Plenty," said Carter.

"Good—let's hustle," said Grandpa, picking up a metal tackle box. He nudged a fat black, orange, and white cat out of the way with his toe, then latched the shed door behind them.

Grandpa Mote, Tyler, and the twins squeezed through

a gap in the back fence where several slats were missing. They picked their way through a brush-covered lot behind the Motes' yard, crossed a dirt road, then plunged into a thicket of pines beyond it.

"Don't fall in the hole," Grandpa Mote warned from his place at the head of the line.

"Hole?" said Tyler, just before he spotted a deep rectangle cut into the ground. It was ringed by young pines and faced with crumbling concrete.

"What is that?" Tyler said to the twins.

"Basement," said Carter.

"Where the old Bailey house used to be," Charlie told Tyler.

"What happened to it?" Tyler wanted to know.

"Hurricane of fifty-eight," Grandpa Mote answered over his shoulder, motioning them along.

"First the wind tore off the top half of the house, and then the tidal wave washed away the rest," said Charlie.

"Were you around for that hurricane, Mr. Mote?" Tyler asked, hurrying to catch up.

But it was Charlie who answered, "You bet he was! He was out at sea on the *Charlotte*—that was the name of his boat—with my dad, who was just a little kid back then."

"Fishing for swordies, we were," Grandpa Mote stuck in.

"When the wind started kicking up, naturally Grandpa didn't head for the harbor," Charlie said. He'd probably heard the story a hundred times, but Tyler could tell it was still just as exciting to him. "It's tons more dangerous for boats to be anchored in a harbor during a hurricane. They get battered against the shoreline."

"Wilbur and I were out there on the water, beyond Gull Island, fighting the wind and the waves for a full day and half the night," said Grandpa Mote. "Wilbur was so slight, I had to knot a line around his waist and rope him to the wheelhouse to keep him from blowing overboard."

"What happened to you when the tidal wave passed by?" Tyler asked.

"Nothing at all," said the twins' grandfather. "At sea, a tidal wave feels like any other storm swell. It's when it hits the shallows near shore that the water piles up."

"And the wave really came all this way inland?" Tyler asked. How far from the bay were they, anyway? He still couldn't see anything but trees.

"Maxine shoved the water right . . . up . . . this inlet," Grandpa Mote said, fighting through an overgrown clump of wild blueberry bushes.

The twins and Tyler pushed their way through the bushes, too, carrying rods and reels and buckets of minnows. Tyler found himself standing on the banks of a shallow inlet that flowed straight out of Badger Bay.

From the bay, up this inlet, to the house back there. . . . Tyler tried to picture the giant wave, suddenly looming darkly over their heads, blocking out the sky.

Then he imagined a million gallons of water smashing down and sweeping away everything. Goose bumps stood up on his arms.

"But Hurricane Fiona's not coming anywhere near here," he said out loud.

"Oh, she's coming, all right," said Grandpa Mote, digging through the tackle box for the correct fishhooks.

"But the weather guys said that Fiona will go ashore somewhere in Maryland," Tyler told him.

Grandpa shook his head as he knotted a hook to the end of Tyler's line.

"You feel it, don't you, Grandpa?" Charlie said knowingly.

"That's right—in my left big toe, the one I mashed with that anchor pretty near fifty years ago," said Grandpa Mote, holding his left boot in the air.

"Grandpa's toe is better than all the weathermen put together," Charlie said proudly, tying on his own hook. "It starts to ache like crazy as much as three days ahead of the storm."

"My toe predicted Maxine in fifty-eight," said Grandpa Mote. "Nobody else did." He handed Tyler back his rod. "Stick a minnow on the hook and drop it in the water. The flukes are down there just waiting to be our dinner."

could tell it was still just as exciting to him. "It's tons more dangerous for boats to be anchored in a harbor during a hurricane. They get battered against the shoreline."

"Wilbur and I were out there on the water, beyond Gull Island, fighting the wind and the waves for a full day and half the night," said Grandpa Mote. "Wilbur was so slight, I had to knot a line around his waist and rope him to the wheelhouse to keep him from blowing overboard."

"What happened to you when the tidal wave passed by?" Tyler asked.

"Nothing at all," said the twins' grandfather. "At sea, a tidal wave feels like any other storm swell. It's when it hits the shallows near shore that the water piles up."

"And the wave really came all this way inland?" Tyler asked. How far from the bay were they, anyway? He still couldn't see anything but trees.

"Maxine shoved the water right . . . up . . . this inlet," Grandpa Mote said, fighting through an overgrown clump of wild blueberry bushes.

The twins and Tyler pushed their way through the bushes, too, carrying rods and reels and buckets of minnows. Tyler found himself standing on the banks of a shallow inlet that flowed straight out of Badger Bay.

From the bay, up this inlet, to the house back there. . . . Tyler tried to picture the giant wave, suddenly looming darkly over their heads, blocking out the sky.

Then he imagined a million gallons of water smashing down and sweeping away everything. Goose bumps stood up on his arms.

"But Hurricane Fiona's not coming anywhere near here," he said out loud.

"Oh, she's coming, all right," said Grandpa Mote, digging through the tackle box for the correct fishhooks.

"But the weather guys said that Fiona will go ashore somewhere in Maryland," Tyler told him.

Grandpa shook his head as he knotted a hook to the end of Tyler's line.

"You feel it, don't you, Grandpa?" Charlie said knowingly.

"That's right—in my left big toe, the one I mashed with that anchor pretty near fifty years ago," said Grandpa Mote, holding his left boot in the air.

"Grandpa's toe is better than all the weathermen put together," Charlie said proudly, tying on his own hook. "It starts to ache like crazy as much as three days ahead of the storm."

"My toe predicted Maxine in fifty-eight," said Grandpa Mote. "Nobody else did." He handed Tyler back his rod. "Stick a minnow on the hook and drop it in the water. The flukes are down there just waiting to be our dinner."

CHAPTER THREE

Dana and Kim got Jake settled under the maple tree in the Meyerses' fenced backyard, along with a bowl of fresh water and a brand-new chew toy.

"He'll be comfortable back here," Kim said to Dana. "It's peaceful, there's plenty of shade and lots of birds for him to watch."

"You behave yourself," Dana told the dog sternly. "We'll be back soon, and maybe we'll bring you a treat."

Jake lay down, rested his head on his forelegs, and sighed.

"Let's bike over to Main Street Sweets," Dana said to Kim.

At the ice-cream shop, the two of them sat on the bench out front and ate double-dip Rocky Roads. Then Dana and Kim pedaled over to Golding's Feed and Seed, where they ended up buying Jake a bag of freeze-dried liver snacks. Then they spent some time looking at the cages full of baby rabbits and chickens for sale. When they finally walked out of the store, Dana noticed that the sky was changing.

"Clouds," she said to Kim. "They're starting to pile up near the horizon."

"It probably just means rain tonight," Kim said with a shrug.

"Unless they're storm clouds ahead of Hurricane Fiona," Dana said.

But Kim shook her head. "Fiona's not coming anywhere near Rockport," she said. "Mom and Dad would know." Mr. and Mrs. Meyers were up-to-date on news because of their TV station.

Dana and Kim turned the corner onto Lilac Place, and Kim said, "Hey, there are a bunch of bikes on my front walk."

"Maybe Tyler rode over," Dana said.

"With the Motes?" said Kim a little uneasily. To her, the Mote twins were still pretty strange.

"Maybe," said Dana, pedaling harder. "Hey, they've got Jake with them."

Her cousin was sitting on the Meyerses' front steps with Jake, one hand on the dog's collar. Jake was panting. Dana could see his pink tongue hanging way out. Charlie and Carter were standing on either side of them.

"Why is he so hot?" Dana called out, jumping her bike onto Kim's sidewalk.

"We caught him running toward the harbor," Tyler said once she'd braked her bike and stepped off.

"The harbor?! How . . . ?" Dana said.

"But Jake was closed up in the backyard!" said Kim.

Dana ran to the side gate. As soon as she opened it, she spotted a sizable mound of dirt near the back fence. Her dog had made his escape by digging out through the Meyerses' flower bed.

"Jake made a huge hole and crawled out," she reported to the group on the steps. "He wrecked some of your flowers, Kim—I'm really sorry. Bad dog," she added to the yellow Lab, who was looking pleased with himself.

"That's okay. We'll buy a few more plants at Griffing Hardware and fix it up before my parents get home," Kim said.

"We'll go with you. We were on our way to Griffing's, too, but we ran into Jake before we got there," Charlie said. "Grandpa's grilling the flukes we caught, and he needs more charcoal."

"What are we going to do about Jake for the next four days?" Dana said, frowning at her dog. "We can't leave him in the backyard by himself, obviously."

"I can't take him with me," Tyler said. "There are bunches of cats at Charlie and Carter's."

Carter nodded. "Fifteen."

"Jake can stay in my bedroom until we get back from Griffing," Kim said. "And then we'll think it."

"Put Jake in the house? But what about your dad?" Dana asked. She knew the reason Kim didn't have any pets was because Mr. Meyers was allergic to animal hair.

"When Dad gets home, we'll set Jake up in the garage," Kim decided. "He won't mess up anything in my room, will he?"

"No, Jake will wait until the door closes, and then he'll stretch out on your bed and be snoring his head off in ten seconds," Tyler replied, laughing, as Dana and Kim led the dog into the house.

A few minutes later, Dana, Kim, Tyler, and the Motes were pedaling down Lilac Place, headed back toward Main Street.

Charlie pointed up at the gathering clouds. "Check out the sky," he said to Tyler. "Grandpa's toe is always right."

" 'Grandpa's toe'?" Dana repeated. The twins said the weirdest things sometimes—or at least Charlie did, because Carter hardly ever said anything at all.

"Grandpa Mote has this big toe that predicts hurricanes days in advance," Tyler explained with a straight face.

"Oh. Sure," said Dana, and Kim rolled her eyes.

Does Tyler really believe that? Dana thought. Still . . . she stared up at the sky herself, and the clouds *did* look twice the size they'd been when she and Kim had ridden home from Golding's.

They're only rain clouds, Dana told herself.

But she wondered about Grandpa Mote's toe, just a little. . . .

CHAPTER FOUR

As soon as Mr. and Mrs. Meyers got home that evening, Dana and Kim made Jake comfortable in the garage. Kim's mom even found an old sofa cushion for him to lie on. When the girls walked back into the living room, Kim's dad had turned on the TV and switched to the Weather Channel. On the screen, a man in a suit was pointing to a map of the eastern United States.

"Looks like Fiona is moving again," Mr. Meyers told them. He sounded concerned.

"Which way is she going?" Dana asked quickly.

"She appears to be heading straight up the coast, which is not good news for us," said Mr. Meyers. "Mary, we could have a serious hurricane on our hands by tomorrow noon!" he called to his wife.

Mrs. Meyers hurried into the living room in time to hear the weather man announce, "Fiona is already packing winds of up to a hundred and five miles an hour, and she seems to be gaining in strength. Hurricane watch is now in effect for all the coastal areas from New Jersey to Cape Cod."

"I'd better fill up the gas tank in the van," Mr. Meyers said. "Every gas station in town ran dry a full day before the last storm hit."

"And we'll have dinner later. We should get to the Harborview Market before they completely sell out of batteries and bottled water," said Mrs. Meyers. "I'll just grab my pocketbook. . . ."

"And buy plenty of masking tape, too," Mr. Meyers said to Kim and Dana. "We might as well start taping the window glass—get a jump on things."

"What about the windows at the lighthouse? And the stranding barn. . . ." Dana was thinking out loud. "What about all the seals?"

Like Ellie, the little blind seal who couldn't ever be released. Ellie had been living at Project Neptune for months, while the Chapins tried to find a permanent home for her. She depended on humans to take care of her. She might be terribly frightened, alone during a storm!

"And Bonnie and Claude, in their outdoor pool," Kim murmured worriedly.

"Dana, I'm certain your parents asked some of the Neptuners to look after things if the storm seemed to be heading this way," Mrs. Meyers said from the front hall.

They probably had, but Dana was still troubled. "I know—I'll call Tim Gilmore when we get back from the store," she said to Kim as they climbed into the backseat of Mrs. Meyers's small car. Tim had been a Neptuner for years, and he was one of the people her folks always turned to in an emergency.

"Yeah, Tim is great," Kim agreed. "He'll have everything under control."

When they got to Ocean Gas, there was already a long line of cars and trucks at the pumps. By the time Mrs. Meyers pulled into the parking lot at the Harborview, next door to Griffing Hardware, almost all of the spaces were filled. And there was pandemonium inside the supermarket itself. People were grabbing stuff off the shelves whether they needed it or not. Dana saw one nervous woman pushing a shopping cart piled with fourteen one-gallon containers of bottled water—Dana counted them.

Mrs. Meyers managed to find four bottles of water hidden in the soda section, and she nabbed the last two packages of A batteries and three packages of D's. "That takes care of our portable radio and some of the flashlights," she said to the girls.

Dana was down on her knees, reaching for three cans of tuna at the back of an almost-empty shelf when Kim whispered, "Wow—everybody in Rockport must be here in the Harborview. There are people I've never even seen before. Like him."

Dana glanced over her shoulder. She saw a small, wrinkled old man with a long white beard and piercing green eyes. Then she noticed Charlie and Carter.

"Hey, Dana!" Charlie called out. "Kim!"

"Hey," Dana said, standing up. She smiled at Carter, too.

"This is our Grandpa Mote," Charlie said proudly, introducing the little old guy.

"I thought it might be," Dana said, shaking hands and trying hard not to stare down at his feet. She wondered which big toe predicted hurricanes, and if it was still aching. Did it hurt more as a storm got closer?

Get a grip! she said to herself. *A toe forecasting the weather?*

But *something* must have been going on inside those work boots, because Grandpa Mote suddenly winced and said, "Yep, this'll be a big un," and he headed for the soda shelves to grab three giant bottles of Coke.

"He means the storm," Charlie said wisely.

"Where's Tyler?" Kim asked, as though she feared for his safety while he was staying with the Motes.

Carter pointed toward the far side of the store. "Buying a throwaway camera," he said.

I guess Tyler's still excited about being in a hurricane. He thinks it'll be fun, like a movie, or a theme-park ride, Dana grumbled to herself.

On the other hand, she didn't want the hurricane to be devastating just to show her cousin up. In fact, Dana would be really happy if Fiona weren't any more dangerous than the wave pool at the water park in Wilton.

The Motes wandered off behind their granddad. Mrs. Meyers, Kim, and Dana hurried to a register to check out, so Dana didn't see Tyler before she left the store.

She and Kim spotted Hallie Wade, though, sitting in her aunt Gretchen's old station wagon in the Harborview parking lot, listening to the car radio. It was always easy to pick Hallie out, because of her bright-red hair.

"The storm's really coming!" she yelled to them through her window. And she seemed as pleased about it as Tyler probably was.

"Tourists," Kim sniffed as she and Dana slid into Mrs. Meyers's car.

Back at the house, they ate a quick dinner of pasta and salad. Then Dana and Kim helped Mr. and Mrs. Meyers make large X's with tape across each window pane. If strong winds broke the glass, the tape would prevent it from blowing into the house and onto them.

When they were finally finished, Dana dialed Tim Gilmore's number. She knew it by heart. It had been posted next to the stranding phone in the lighthouse for years.

The phone rang twice before Tim's answering machine picked up: "This is Tim. To all Neptuners—I'll be at the Point on Wednesday evening for as long as it takes. Join me, okay? Anyone else, please leave a message."

"Hi, Tim, this is Dana. Just checking," Dana said into the phone before she hung up.

"He's on the case, right?" Kim said, standing beside her in the Meyerses' kitchen.

"Yeah, he's there," Dana said, "and a bunch of other

Neptuners probably will be, too, after they hear his message."

"So there's nothing to worry about," Kim said.

Nothing except a 105 mile-an-hour wind, Dana said to herself. *Not to mention tidal surges.*

But there was nothing Tim Gilmore and all of the Neptuners in the world could do about *that*.

"You girls had better get to bed," Mrs. Meyers told them. "Tomorrow could be a very long day."

CHAPTER FIVE

The inside of the Motes' house wasn't at all like what Tyler had imagined. Okay, maybe it could have used another coat of paint and some more furniture. But it was as neat and clean as Dr. Bucalo's examining room at the Point.

"Dad says he wants this place to look as trim as an Army barracks," Charlie explained. "He says when three guys live together, things can get out of hand really fast. So everybody has chores. Like I dust and pick up stuff. Carter vacuums, because he knows how to fix the motor when it breaks."

"We both wash dishes," Carter added.

"And when Dad's home, he washes clothes," said Charlie.

The twins' room was upstairs under the eaves, high enough for them to see all the way to the harbor.

"Cool!" said Tyler, peering out the window at the boats tied up at Halstead's Wharf.

"Yeah, we can usually spot the *Bonnie Jean* when she's leaving the wharf or coming back to anchor," Charlie said.

There was a huge, slightly faded, stuffed swordfish on one wall. "From Grandpa," said Carter.

Another wall was covered with pictures Carter had drawn: of Grandpa Mote fishing at the inlet; of the twins' dad on the deck of the *Bonnie Jean;* of their seventh-grade math teacher, Mr. Jackson, looking disgusted; of Charlie surrounded by cats. There was even a view from the lighthouse at Parsons Point, with harbor seals hauled out on Gull Island, fishing boats bobbing through the swells, and a humpback whale spouting in the distance.

One of the first things Tyler thought about when he woke up in the middle of the night was saving those pictures, because he realized that it was raining hard outside and that, somehow, his face was getting awfully wet indoors.

The twins had set up a cot between their beds for Tyler to sleep on. Unfortunately for him, his head was directly under a major leak in the Motes' roof. That wasn't the only leak, though. Tyler could hear other drips, even over the drumming of the rain. And the whistling of the wind.

Is the storm here already? he said to himself.

The room was pitch-black. Tyler couldn't see anything. He pushed himself off the cot, took one step, and fell over Charlie's bed.

"Ooof . . . wh-what's going on?" Charlie said groggily.

"It's raining in here," Tyler told him. "Where's the light switch?"

"Raining?" said Carter, waking up quickly.

"It's on the left side of the door. . . ." Charlie hopped out of his bed and flipped the switch himself. The three of them blinked in the brightness.

"Whoa!" Charlie said as they looked around the room.

Now the drip above Tyler's cot was more like a steady stream. There was another leak in the corner near the window and a third and fourth much too close to Carter's drawings.

"Wind blew shingles loose," said Carter.

"Carter, move your pictures," Charlie said to his brother, and he pulled the cot away from the drip. "Tyler and I'll get some buckets."

They felt their way down the stairs, to find Grandpa Mote sitting in the lighted kitchen with all the cats.

"Leaks in our room," Charlie said to him, starting to dig around in the cabinets.

Grandpa Mote just nodded. "It'll get a lot worse before it gets better," he said.

"Is this it, Mr. Mote?" Tyler asked him. "Is this Fiona?"

Grandpa Mote shook his head. "Just a preview," he said. "But she's on her way, for sure."

Lightning flashed, lighting up the backyard long enough for Tyler to see tree limbs swaying. Some of the Motes' cats were trembling. They didn't like the storm, not even from the safety of the kitchen.

"What about Dad? Do you think he'll stay out on the *Bonnie Jean* until the storm's passed?" Charlie said to his grandfather. So far he'd found two buckets, a cooking pot, and a blue plastic bowl.

"Be the smartest thing," Grandpa Mote replied. "Your dad's got young Freddy Marder helping him on the boat. They'll be all right, just like we were in fifty-eight."

Charlie nodded. "Yeah, Dad'll be all right," he repeated. But Tyler thought he sounded pretty worried.

Tyler and Charlie climbed back up the stairs. They stuck the buckets and pots under the drips in the twins' bedroom, mopped up the water on Tyler's cot with a towel, and crawled back into bed. But Tyler didn't have much luck sleeping. And Carter must have been having a nightmare, because he kept muttering, "It's coming, it's coming!"

As soon as it grew light, Tyler slipped out of bed and tiptoed over to the window.

The sun was completely hidden by clouds. The sky was a flat, solid gray. So was the water in the harbor, except for the ruffles of white on the waves smacking against the hulls of boats tied up at the wharf.

Carter joined him at the window. "There's already a lot of wind," he murmured. "What'll happen when the real storm gets here?"

A limb of an oak tree whacked against the house, and Charlie sat straight up in bed. Then the three boys got dressed and went down to the kitchen for cereal, but Grandpa Mote was already cooking pancakes. Tyler noticed he'd taped a lot of the downstairs windows. He probably hadn't slept at all.

"What should we be doing?" Charlie asked his granddad.

"Eat your pancakes," Grandpa Mote said, handing each of the boys a big stack on a plate. "We may have to cut the gas off—this could be our last hot meal for a while."

They'd barely sat down at the table, though, when Grandpa Mote took a yellow slicker off the hook beside the back door.

"Where are you going?" Carter said.

"Over to my house, make sure everything's tied down," his granddad said.

"We'll go with you," said Charlie, shoving his chair back.

But Grandpa Mote shook his head. "You stay here until I come back," he said.

"Why aren't you taking Old Blue?" Carter asked.

That's what the twins called Grandpa Mote's old Toyota truck, parked down the street on a rise in the road.

"It'd just get stuck in the mud," said their grandfather. "Tape the rest of the windows."

He pulled open the back door. Rain gusted into the kitchen, and cats scattered everywhere.

As soon as Grandpa Mote jerked the door closed behind him, Tyler and the twins ran to a window. They watched him hurrying toward the gap in the back fence, bent almost double in the rain.

"Where's his house?" Tyler said to the twins.

"On the far side of the inlet, and then some," said Carter forlornly.

The pancakes were delicious, but none of them had much of an appetite. *The hurricane isn't even here yet, and already there's nothing fun about it,* Tyler said to himself.

They washed and dried their dishes and put them away. They were on their way upstairs to tape windows and check on the buckets and bowls catching rainwater when there was a loud rattle at the front of the house.

"What was that?" Tyler said to Charlie.

"The wind blowing against the door?" Charlie answered.

But Carter said, "Uh-uh—somebody's knocking."

When they opened the front door, Dana was standing on the Motes' porch, looking half drowned. She was wearing a waterproof windbreaker. But her wet hair was plastered to her head, her jeans were soaked, and her sneakers were coated with mud. Dana's eyes were red, as though she might have been crying.

Tyler was amazed to see her out in the storm. "What are you doing here?" he said to his cousin, spotting her bike leaning against the gate.

"Come inside," said Charlie, pulling her into the house and closing the front door. Water was streaming off her onto the floor.

"What's wrong?" said Carter.

"It's . . . it's Jake!" Dana said, a catch in her voice. "He's gone!"

"How?" said Tyler. "When did—"

"He spent the night in the garage," Dana said, trying hard not to burst into tears. "Only Mr. Meyers got up really early this morning because he suddenly remembered a bird feeder in the backyard that he was afraid might blow away. He forgot all about Jake being asleep on the sofa cushion. He flipped open the garage door, ran around the house to get the bird feeder . . ."

"And Jake got out," Tyler said.

"Right, without Mr. Meyers even seeing him. When Kim's folks got ready to leave for work, they realized Jake was gone. So he's been wandering around in this weather for a couple of hours at least," Dana said, tears welling up in her eyes.

"Are the Meyerses out looking for him?" Tyler asked her.

"Uh-uh. They had to get to the TV station and start broadcasting hurricane information," Dana said. "They called the police station and told them to be on the alert for a yellow Lab. But the police have too much other stuff on their minds right now!"

She added, "Your phone isn't working."

"I bet it was that branch that crashed against the house," Charlie guessed. "It probably knocked down the phone line."

"So I rode over here," Dana said. "Kim's staying at her house in case anybody calls about Jake. Will you help me?"

"What are we waiting for?" said Tyler. Jake was practically his dog, too.

Carter said, "Let's do it!" He liked Dana a lot.

"What about Grandpa? He told us not to move until he gets back," Charlie reminded his brother. "And we have to tape the rest of the windows . . . Okay"—he'd decided in a heartbeat—"I'll stay here, tape the windows, write a note for Grandpa, and catch up with you."

"Great!" said Tyler, throwing open the door again. The rain was coming down in sheets. "Uh . . . got an extra slicker?" he added.

CHAPTER SIX

"I think we should look for Jake near the harbor," Tyler yelled over the wind. "That's where he was headed when we found him yesterday."

Tyler, Dana, and Carter were standing in the rain in front of the Motes' house with their bikes, trying to decide which way to go first.

Tyler was wearing an old gray slicker that had belonged to the twins' mom. Carter had on his dad's green poncho, about ten sizes too big for him. He kept pushing back the hood, because it fell forward and covered his face. And Dana had a garbage-bag scarf wrapped around her head, rigged up by Charlie to keep some of the rain off.

"Let's just get started!" Dana said, steering her bike through the gate.

The three of them pedaled up Roanoke Avenue, the wind blasting them with rain from the side. Then it swung around and drenched them from the front. It was hard to hold their bikes steady. Plus it had rained so much that the water wasn't draining away from the road. They rolled into a giant puddle that covered their bike wheels almost to the hubs. And when they turned onto Main Street, closer to the harbor, the water got even deeper.

"It's not just from the rain. Wind's already shoving seawater ashore," Carter told Tyler and Dana.

Main Street was deserted. Besides them, there were no people—or dogs—crazy enough to brave the weather. There wasn't even a seagull to be seen, although there was usually a crowd of them shrieking overhead.

Except for Griffing Hardware—and Mr. Griffing happened to live in an apartment at the back—all the stores were closed and dark, their windows taped or boarded up. The wind seemed to be growing stronger, slamming signs back and forth and bending tree branches until they looked ready to break.

"This is like pedaling through rubber cement," Dana said breathlessly from the middle of a lake in front of Main Street Sweets. She stepped off her bike and starting pushing it forward.

So did Carter, then Tyler. The three of them sloshed through water over their knees. Tyler was so wet anyhow that he hardly noticed.

He wiped the rain out of his eyes and stared toward the ice cream shop. The water was almost up to the threshold there. With any more rain, or a higher wind,

Main Street Sweets would be flooded. So would Herb's Meats and Catering, and Kathleen's Bakery just beyond it. And what about the stores next to the wharf, like Rockport Fuel and Bait? They were probably under water already.

A small kid could drown here, Tyler said to himself. Or a small dog. Luckily, Jake was a retriever—he'd been bred to swim.

Suddenly Carter had an idea. "What about the Dumpster at Seafood Grill?"

"Yeah, every cat in Rockport goes there to eat, and half the dogs, too," said Tyler.

"Jake hasn't eaten since last night, so he must be hungry," Dana added, brightening a little. "With all the leftovers they throw away at the grill . . ."

The three of them pushed on, until they'd reached the restaurant not far from Halstead's Wharf. The red neon lobster in the front window of the grill still glowed cheerfully. But Tyler said, "Check out that water!" It had risen several inches over the threshold, to lap against the big oak doors.

"Jake can't be here. The Dumpster in back must be floating by now!" Dana said hopelessly.

"Let's look anyway," said Tyler, trying not to sound discouraged himself. He leaned his bike against a planter and slogged on. Carter and Dana followed him toward the back of the building.

"Wow!" Tyler murmured, stopping short.

A solid sheet of water stretched from the corner of

the Seafood Grill all the way down to the harbor. It was covered with little whitecaps churned up by the high wind. Only the tops of the wooden planks that formed Halstead's Wharf broke the surface. And all the boats usually berthed there were gone.

They're all riding out the storm at sea, Tyler guessed, *like Mr. Mote.*

"*Somebody's* here," Carter said from behind him.

"In all this water? Who?" said Dana, wading up beside Tyler. "Oh, it's just a bike."

"It's Hallie's bike!" Carter said.

Tyler recognized it, too, as soon as he saw it propped against the Dumpster, only the top of its frame above water. It was Hallie Wade's shiny green mountain bike, the one her great-aunt Gretchen had bought for her a couple of months ago.

"Why would she leave it here?" he shouted into the wind, glancing around uneasily. It wouldn't be that hard to get swept into the bay. . . .

"Who ever knows with Hallie!" Dana yelled back, shrugging.

Dana and Hallie didn't exactly see eye to eye, but Tyler sort of liked her. Hallie was always up for anything. And she was friends with the Mote twins—she'd hung out with them in the summertime for years. Plus she had lots of the same feelings about wild animals and their right to live free as Tyler did.

"Anyway, Jake's not around," Dana was saying.

"Today we're more likely to run into a seal down here than a dog. Let's get our bikes and get going."

She turned toward Main Street again.

But a voice shouted, "Hey!"

"Where's that coming from?" Tyler said to Carter.

"Don't know," Carter said.

Suddenly a figure in a blue poncho rose up inside the Dumpster. "Hey, don't just stand there—I could use some help!"

It was Hallie! And she was holding something small, close to her body.

Tyler and Carter waded over to the Dumpster. The water was up to their thighs now.

"What are you doing in there?" Tyler said to Hallie.

"You want to climb down?" Carter asked her.

"*I* can climb down," Hallie said. "I rode to the harbor to see the storm up close, and I found . . . Hold these for me."

She leaned over the edge of the Dumpster to hand Tyler what could have been a fuzzy, light-colored rag.

But it wasn't a rag at all. It was warm, solid, and it wriggled. It also mewed. "It's a kitten!" Tyler said, looking down at the tiny reddish animal. Its eyes were barely open, and it was soaking wet and very unhappy. It hissed, and struggled in Tyler's grasp.

"Two kittens," Hallie said, handing Carter a black one before she jumped down from the Dumpster herself. She landed with a splash in the water. "I heard them crying. They're probably not more than a week or so old," she said. "I guess their mother carried them into the Dumpster for safekeeping, and then couldn't get back to them when the water rose."

Hallie took the reddish kitten from Tyler, stretched out the neck of her pink T-shirt, and dropped the kitten inside it. "They'll warm up next to my skin," she said, dropping Carter's kitten down her shirt as well. "I'll take them home and put them on a heating pad. And feed them with an eyedropper. What are you guys doing here, anyway?" she asked them then. "Did you come to see the storm, too?"

"No," Dana said with a sigh. "Jake ran away from the Meyerses' house, and we're looking for him."

"Wow, your dog's lost?" said Hallie. "Wait a minute . . . I saw a yellow Lab about half an hour ago. I never thought about it being Jake, not in Rockport."

"You did? Where?" Dana said urgently.

"I watched him swim across that big puddle at the start of Main Street," Hallie said. "When he got to the far side, he headed straight up Harbor Lane."

"Oh, no." Dana groaned. "I'll bet he was on his way home!"

"Then he'll be okay—it's only five miles," Tyler said. He'd seen Jake cover ten miles without tiring plenty of times, running along the shore of the bay to keep up with their kayaks.

"Tim or another Neptuner will let him into the stranding barn," Tyler went on.

"*If* he makes it!" Dana said. "And what if there

aren't any Neptuners at the Point right now? Maybe Tim's getting his own house ready for Fiona."

"If the wind's strong enough, it can blow away a car," Carter added in a low voice.

A car? Tyler said to himself, and he and Dana looked at each other. At the Point there was no protection from the wind—Jake might be blown right into the ocean!

"Harbor Lane follows the edge of the bay . . . so it must be as flooded as this is," Hallie said slowly.

Tyler made up his mind. "I'll go after him," he said. "Dana, you ride back to the Meyerses' and try to call Tim. Carter, go home before Charlie comes looking for us in town. And Hallie, you'd better take the kittens to your aunt's—"

"No way!" Dana interrupted. She started wading toward their bikes. "I'm responsible for Jake—I'll find him!"

"I'm going with you, too," Hallie said to Tyler. "The kittens are warming up. They're not even mewing now. We'll feed them at the Point—you guys are used to feeding orphan animals."

"The more of us, the better," Carter said.

Tyler nodded. "The four of us can make it—definitely," he said.

CHAPTER SEVEN

Dana couldn't have felt any worse if she'd lost Jake herself. All she could think about was getting to the lighthouse and finding him waiting!

On a regular day she and Tyler could bike from downtown Rockport to the Point in less than half an hour. But that Thursday was definitely not a regular day. Dana checked her watch when she, Tyler, Carter, and Hallie left the parking lot of the Seafood Grill: it was 9:42. Twenty minutes later, they'd barely reached the outskirts of town.

The wind was even stronger, whipping the rain into Dana's eyes and often making it impossible for her to see more than a few feet in front of her handlebars. It had been hard enough to retrace their route down Main Street. But once they turned onto Harbor Lane, the water that covered the road was actually flowing like a river.

"This looks kind of iffy," Hallie shouted over the

wind. She braked her bike to adjust the kittens inside her T-shirt.

"The wind's pushing in the tide from the bay!" said Carter, stopping, too.

Usually calm and unruffled, Badger Bay had been stirred into a foamy, white froth that was streaming across the road.

"There's no way around, is there?" Tyler asked Carter.

But Dana wasn't willing to waste a single second. "I'm going ahead!" she said, jumping off her bike and shoving it forward, into the water.

Right away, she felt a powerful current swirling against her legs, threatening to trip her or to wrench the bike away from her.

Then Carter caught up with her and grabbed one of her handlebars, holding his own bike steady with his other hand. "Just keep moving," he said to Dana.

They made it safely to the far side of the pool of surging seawater. Tyler and Hallie crossed it together as well. Before the four of them rode on, Dana spotted an elderly woman tying a rowboat to her front porch, preparing for the worst.

They passed a couple of cars on the shoulder of the road, stalled by the weather. A man was tinkering with the engine of one of them, using the hood as a shelter from the rain and wind.

As the kids struggled past him, he raised his head to

yell, "You'd better get home before the road washes out!"

"We're trying to!" Dana yelled back, pedaling as hard as she could.

But she wasn't gaining much ground—the wind kept pushing her sideways. Plus, they were all being pelted with bits of bark and shredded leaves ripped off trees and bushes. They stung Dana's face, and made her eyes water.

She didn't know if it was her imagination or if the heavy pedaling was heating her up, but the air felt much warmer to her. She was sweating under Kim's windbreaker.

A few seconds later, Hallie yelled, "Is it just me, or is it getting steamy out here?"

And Tyler yelled, "Hurricanes are tropical, right? Maybe it's pulling along hot air from the south!"

Which probably means Fiona's a lot closer now, Dana said to herself. She stood up on her pedals to push even harder.

"Look out!" Carter shouted suddenly.

A large piece of flattened metal went spinning past them to land with a splash in a water-filled ditch farther up the road.

Pedaling when they could, or running alongside their bikes, they forded two more flowing lakes, dodged scraps of airborne lumber, and came across half a dozen stalled cars. They even spotted some seagulls flying backward, caught in the gale.

Almost an hour passed before they reached the turnoff to the Point. Peering through a curtain of rain, Dana shouted to the others in disbelief: "We actually made it!"

"Wow—listen to the mailboxes!" Tyler said from behind her.

There was a row of metal mailboxes at the head of their gravel road, for their own mail as well as for Project Neptune's. The wind was rattling them like snare drums!

"Can you see anybody?" Carter called out to Dana.

Dana shook her head. "Nothing but rain!" she replied.

She was exhausted from the journey. But just turning onto their road made Dana feel a thousand times better—she was home. And she hoped more than anything that her dog was there, too.

Dana was focusing on the lighthouse as she pushed her bike forward. She was looking for the patch of light yellow that might be Jake.

It was Tyler who noticed some of the damage the wind had already done at the Point. "The roof's coming off the food-prep shed!" he shouted. "A piece of it's already gone, and—"

"There it is!" said Hallie, pointing up the road.

A large, ragged section of boards and shingles had been ripped off the shed and tossed onto the gravel road. Dana glanced toward the stranding barn, concerned that it might be coming apart, too, with a bunch of frightened seals caged inside. Then she remembered Bonnie and Claude. As she glanced quickly toward the dolphin pool, she spotted a blue truck parked at the side of the barn.

That's Tim Gilmore's truck! she said to herself, hugely relieved. *Maybe Tim found Jake!*

Then Hallie yelled, "Somebody's under those boards—I see boots!"

And Dana's heart plummeted to her feet. *It must be Tim,* she told herself.

Dana, Tyler, Hallie, and Carter dropped their bikes and ran toward the heavy piece of roofing lying on the gravel road. It was about three feet by four feet. It covered the person underneath it almost completely.

"Work boots," said Carter.

"I think it might be Tim Gilmore," Dana told them woefully, squatting down beside his legs. "His truck's parked near the barn. Tim?" she said loudly.

But the still figure didn't budge.

Hallie arranged the kittens inside her shirt again and knelt down to try to look under the boards. "It is Tim. I see part of his mustache," she said.

"We have to lift this thing off him," Tyler said, grabbing a corner of the roofing.

Hallie said, "If we drop it, we might hurt him even more than he already—"

"So we *won't* drop it!" said Dana. They had to know the worst.

Carter nodded, and Hallie stood up to help, too.

"On three," Tyler told them. "One . . . two . . ."—Dana took a deep breath—"three!" Tyler said.

All of them lifted. The boards were water soaked and heavy, but the kids managed to hold on even as the wind tried to wrestle with them.

"Walk forward . . . ," Tyler huffed.

Once the roofing had cleared Tim's head safely, the four of them lowered it onto the gray rocks of the Point. Then they took a closer look at Tim.

He was lying on his stomach, one of his arms thrown up over his head, the other down by his side. His legs were stretched straight out.

"He's breathing okay," Dana said thankfully.

"His arm's bleeding, but I don't think it's broken or anything," Tyler said, bending down close to it.

"His legs look okay, too," said Carter. He was trying to keep the rain off Tim with his own poncho.

"But he's got a giant gash in the back of his head," Hallie said, pointing. The wet hair around it was matted with blood.

"The piece of roof flew through the air, hit him in the head, and knocked him unconscious," Dana guessed. How long had Tim been lying there?

"We have to move him," said Tyler.

"No! In first-aid classes, they always warn you not to move anybody until a doctor checks 'em out," Hallie said.

"What doctor? A hurricane's coming!" said Carter.

"A doctor wouldn't be able to get to the Point now even if our phone's working, which it probably isn't," Dana said. "I'll bring a tarp from the stranding barn," she told Tyler. "We'll move Tim like the Neptuners moved Bonnie and Claude from the beach."

"Just hurry!" said Tyler.

Dana slid open the side door of the stranding barn and stepped quietly through it, out of the rain. It was dark inside the barn. When Dana flipped the light switch, nothing happened. She realized the filters weren't gurgling in the fiberglass exercise pools, either.

We've already lost electricity, Dana thought.

The wind was whistling through cracks in the old siding, and rain pounded against the roof. Dana peered toward the wire cages lining the walls. In several of them, seals' eyes glowed as they watched her silently. Ellie, the blind grey seal, wriggled excitedly in her cage. She'd recognized Dana's scent. Dana reached in to touch Ellie's head and reassure her. Suddenly there was a *crack!* of lightning not far away, followed quickly by a rumble of thunder.

That was a little too close! Dana said to herself. She ran to the supply cabinet, pulled out a canvas tarp, and rushed back outside.

She, Tyler, Carter, and Hallie spread the tarp out right next to Tim. Then, carefully, they rolled him over onto it.

Each of them picked up a corner of the tarp.

"Hold his head off the ground," Dana said to Hallie. They were hanging on to the top two corners of the tarp. "Let's get him inside in a hurry."

The gravel road was rough going. But once they'd pulled Tim's tarp onto the smooth, wet rocks of the Point, it practically glided along. In a couple of minutes, they were standing beside the steep back steps of the lighthouse.

"Now what?" Hallie said to Dana. "Tim's too heavy for you and me to pull straight up these steps."

"Carter can help on this end. Tyler, you just make sure Tim doesn't roll out," Dana said.

Carter joined Dana and Hallie on the bottom step, and all three of them tugged on the tarp, but they couldn't seem to budge Tim more than a few inches.

Suddenly another lightning bolt arced through the clouds. It crackled to the ground at the tip of the Point. The thunder was immediate and deafening.

Dana pulled with all her strength, and Hallie and Carter must have been encouraged by the lightning, too, because all at once Tim's tarp slid up the wooden steps. Now Tim was lying on the back porch.

Dana pushed the back door open, ready to shove the kitchen table out of the way. But the instant she stepped inside the darkened kitchen, something crashed against her, hard, practically taking her breath away. There was a joyful bark.

"Jake!" Dana shrieked. "You're here!" Tim must have put Jake in the house. He'd probably gotten hit in the head when he was on his way back to the stranding barn.

"Settle down," Dana said to the delighted yellow Lab. "We have work to do."

She and Tyler and the others dragged Tim's tarp across the kitchen and straight into the living room. They rolled him onto the soft hooked rug that Dana's grandmother had made before Dana was born.

"Hey, I think his eyes are moving," Hallie said.

Dana stared into Tim's face, and saw his eyelids flicker a few times. Then, all at once, Tim's eyes opened!

"What . . . ," Tim said, looking up at the dog and the kids gathered around him. "What happened? What are you guys doing here?"

"Looking for Jake," Dana said, her arm around her dog.

Tim tried to raise himself onto his elbows, but Hallie pushed him gently back down. "You ought to stay still for a while," she told him.

"How did I get into the house?" Tim asked. He touched his head, and winced.

"Part of the shed roof sneaked up on you," Dana told him.

"And we pulled you into the house before you drowned out there," Tyler added with a grin.

Tim felt well enough to grin back.

He's going to be okay, Dana thought. "Thanks for finding Jake for us, Tim," she added out loud. To herself she said, *Now all we have to do is live through Fiona!*

 **CHAPTER EIGHT**

"So what do we do next?" said Tyler, patting Jake's head.

He was dead tired, and he knew what he'd like to do—crawl into bed and take a long, peaceful nap.

But that isn't exactly an option in a hurricane, he said to himself, slipping out of his rain gear.

"I know what *I* have to do," Hallie said, pulling her own poncho off over her head. "Catch 'em before they drop, okay?" she told Carter and Tyler.

She meant the kittens. Tyler could see their small, wriggling bodies under Hallie's T-shirt, just above the waist of her shorts.

"And keep an eye on Jake, just in case he thinks they're mice or something," Hallie added.

Dana grabbed Jake's collar.

Slowly, Hallie pulled the hem of her shirt out of her waistband.

"Got one!" Carter said as the black kitten tumbled out first.

Tyler caught the red one. "This guy looks okay," he said, stroking the kitten as he mewed hungrily. "He's warm and not even very rained on."

"Thanks," Hallie said, taking the red kitten from Tyler. "Does anybody know what baby kittens eat?" she asked.

"Sure, I do," said Carter. He'd had plenty of experience with cats of all ages.

"There's milk in the kitchen," Dana told them.

"And eggs?" said Carter.

"Yep, and clean eyedroppers on the bottom shelf of the white cabinet," Tim said from the floor. Neptuners were always needing eyedroppers. "And check on the phone, okay?"

Hallie and Carter headed for the kitchen with the kittens.

"We've got to get ready for Fiona," Tim said to the cousins. "I've taped the windows in the house."

Tyler glanced around the living room and saw neat X's of masking tape on each of the panes.

"But I didn't make it to the clinic or the barn. Or the food-prep shed." Then Tim touched his head, remembering what had hit him. "With half the roof gone, I guess we don't need to bother about taping the windows in the shed," he added, trying again to sit up.

Dana pushed him back down. "You might have a concussion. You shouldn't be moving around," she told him firmly. "We'll get you some dry clothes, though. Tyler and I'll bring some of Dad's stuff down, and Tyler can help you change. And, Tim—thanks for finding Jake for us."

"Thanks for finding *me*," Tim said.

"The phone's not working," Hallie called from the kitchen. Which wasn't a surprise to anybody.

Jake followed Tyler and Dana upstairs, unwilling to let them out of his sight. In Uncle Joe's closet, the cousins found a pair of sweatpants and an old cotton shirt that buttoned up the front—easy to put on, even for someone lying on the floor. They grabbed a blanket for Tim, too, and Dana's portable radio, and started downstairs with Jake at their heels.

"While you're helping Tim, I'll take care of the clinic and the stranding barn," Dana told Tyler.

"No way you're going out there alone!" said Tyler. "Carter can help Tim."

"But . . . okay," Dana agreed pretty quickly.

Hallie was sitting at the table in the kitchen, making the kittens comfortable in a big bread basket lined with towels. Carter was warming a milk-and-egg mixture on the stove for them to eat.

"Carter, could you get Tim into these dry clothes? We're going out to tape windows and check on the animals," Dana said, setting the radio down on the table.

"I'll go with you!" Hallie said, jumping to her feet.

"Uh-uh," Tyler said. "Two of us can keep track of each other out there—three people is one too many."

He expected Hallie to argue, but she glanced at him

and then at Dana and didn't insist. Instead, she switched on the radio and tuned in to SHOR-FM, Rockport.

Over the static, the announcer was saying, ". . . winds already in excess of a hundred miles an hour . . ."

Hallie filled an eyedropper and picked up the red kitten. "There's a lot of stuff flying around out there," she told the cousins. "Watch out."

"Yeah, okay." Tyler grabbed a big roll of tape that Tim had left on the counter and tucked it under his belt. "Ready?" he said to Dana, pulling on the old gray slicker again. "Don't you want to get your own poncho?"

Dana shook her head. "What for? I'm already soaked."

"Hey, guys—this is *not* a good idea!" Tim called from the rug on the living-room floor. "You could get hurt, and Joe and Lissa would never—"

But Tyler interrupted him. "There are two of us, Tim. We'll be looking out for each other."

"Let's go, Tyler," said Dana.

Carter was hanging on to Jake. "You're staying with us, boy," he told the dog.

Tyler turned the knob on the back door, and it opened with a *pop* that made Jake bark.

"Pressure's dropping way down. Fiona's definitely here," Carter said gravely.

A wind gust smashed the door into Tyler's shoulder, pushing him back. Rain blasted into the kitchen. Tyler lowered his head and charged onto the back porch, with Dana right behind him.

"Open some windows in the barn—pressure!" Carter shouted to them, just before the door banged closed.

"Wow!" Tyler yelled into the roaring gale. "Check that out!"

There were only a few scrawny pine trees on the Point, growing in what seemed to be solid rock. The one closest to the lighthouse had been wrenched out by its roots, and the wind was tumbling it closer and closer to the cliffs.

"Look at the ocean!" Dana yelled in his ear.

The Atlantic was one gigantic, angry whitecap for as far as Tyler could see.

I feel sorry for anybody on a boat out there, Tyler murmured. And then he reminded himself about Mr. Mote, riding out the storm on the *Bonnie Jean. Carter— and Charlie—must really be worried,* he said to himself.

"I hope the barn holds together!" Dana shouted.

The stranding barn appeared to be rocking on its foundation. On the roof, a large panel of shingles was flapping wildly in the wind.

"Let's get moving!" Tyler said, starting down the steps.

He and Dana had had some protection from the storm while they were standing on the back porch. When they left the side of the house, though, the wind hit Tyler so hard that it took his breath away. It also threatened to knock him down and maybe tumble him toward the cliffs as easily as the pine tree!

"Crawl!" Dana shouted, dropping to her hands and knees.

She was right—the wind didn't have as much to work with if they stayed low. Tyler and Dana scurried across the rocks like two frightened crabs, until they reached the door of Dr. Bucalo's clinic.

The small building was low, too, and built of brick. It stood solid as a rock. But once the cousins edged inside, into the front room, they discovered a couple of broken panes and a mess of shattered glass and water. Rain was pouring onto the floor near Dr. Bucalo's computer.

Tyler jerked its plug out of the socket, and Dana rolled the computer away from the window. They stowed it in the supply closet. Then they pushed open the door to the recovery room.

India was a baby harbor seal that a Neptuner had found washed up on Indian Beach. She was lying on her side in her cage, her round head resting against the wires.

"She looks all right," Tyler whispered to Dana.

When she'd come to the Point several weeks before, India had been so thin that all her ribs showed, her fur was dull and patchy, and she'd had a lung infection. Now she was plump and shiny. Her stiff white whiskers twitched as she sniffed the air for food.

"She should be fed again this evening—all the animals should," Dana whispered worriedly.

Tyler nodded. Not only did they have the storm to get through, but the supply of frozen fish in the food-prep shed would spoil without electricity. What would the seals, and Bonnie and Claude, eat after the storm moved on?

"Wow—Bonnie and Claude," Tyler repeated out loud, listening to the wind raging around the clinic.

"Yeah, I know," Dana said. "But we can't do anything for them right now."

They *could* do something about the clinic, though. Before they left, they pulled the metal bottom off an empty cage and found a hammer and nails in the supply closet. They nailed the metal across the broken window to keep most of the rain out.

Then Tyler and Dana scrambled over the rocks to the stranding barn, keeping an eye on the loose panel of roof shingles until they were safely indoors again. None of the barn windows had broken. Maybe it was because they were small, and the old glass in them was thick.

Once the cousins had taped the panes, they took some time to check on the seals. There were several harbor seal colonies near Parsons Point, so many of Project Neptune's seal rescues involved harbor seals. That day there were nine of them recovering in the barn, and Conan, the largest, was ready to be released. Months before, he'd swallowed plastic garbage floating in the ocean, confusing it with squid, his real food. The plastic had filled up his stomach and he'd almost died of starvation before he was saved by some Neptuners.

"I'm really glad Mom and Dad didn't have time to turn Conan loose on Perth Island before they left for California," Dana whispered to Tyler as they glanced into his cage.

"Yeah, who knows what Fiona's doing to the harbor seal colonies right now?" Tyler whispered back.

Harbor seals on the East Coast gave birth in May, so there were lots of baby seals swimming around in the Atlantic at this time of year. *Are they strong enough to ride out a hurricane?* he wondered.

All the seals in the barn were restless, even Ellie. Raised up on their front flippers, they were swaying back and forth in their cages, snuffling nervously through the wires that enclosed them.

"They're scared of the wind," Tyler murmured to Dana.

"Who wouldn't be? Let's just hope the roof stays on," Dana replied, then added, "We should get back to the lighthouse before somebody comes looking for us."

Suddenly there was a terrific tearing noise. Seconds later, something smacked into the outside of the barn.

"I guess those shingles are history," Tyler said. Rain started streaming down into the exercise pools in the center of the barn.

Dana walked to the door, ready to slide it open. But it wouldn't budge.

"I can't move it," she said to Tyler.

"Let me try," Tyler said. He jiggled the door a little, then shoved it, hard. "It's . . . like . . . something's holding it closed," he puffed.

Shrugging, Dana said, "We'll use the door on the far side."

"It's way too close to the cliffs," Tyler warned. They could end up in the Atlantic!

"We'll stay low and hang on to the barn," said Dana.

She pulled open the door and disappeared around it before Tyler could say anything else. He had to follow her.

This has to be the worst of the storm! he thought as soon as he stepped outside. There was so much water in the air that he could almost have been swimming! But at the same time, it felt as though a giant hand were trying to push him through the side of the barn.

Better than getting shoved toward the ocean, he told himself. Not more than fifteen feet away, sheer stone cliffs dropped seventy feet straight down into the churning Atlantic.

Tyler crouched even lower and inched forward, the top half of his body spread-eagled against the wooden siding. He wished his fingers were suction cups!

Out of the corner of his eye, Tyler could see that Dana was moving along more quickly than he was. She was eager to reach the corner of the barn so that she could turn away from the wind and the cliffs.

Suddenly, the wind swirled from the opposite direction.

Tyler heard a terrified scream!

He glanced toward his cousin again, and saw her lying on her back on the ground a couple of feet away from the barn. Her fingers clutched frantically at the slick gray rocks beneath her.

But Fiona was pushing Dana, slowly but surely, toward the cliffs and the raging Atlantic Ocean!

CHAPTER NINE

One second Dana was edging along the water-soaked siding of the stranding barn, keeping her body as low and as flat as she could and breathing through her mouth because it was raining so hard. The next second, her left foot slipped and she lost her balance and fell backward into a monster wind gust that pushed her down onto the rocks!

Dana screamed and tried desperately to grab hold of something, anything—a weed or a few blades of salt grass. But the rocks of the Point were bare, wet, and slippery. Dana could feel herself sliding, little by little, toward the cliffs and the mountainous waves below!

Now I'm going to die, Dana thought, closing her eyes against the rain. Fiona was going to kill her, and there was nothing she could do about it.

Wham! Something fell across Dana's legs with such force that for a moment she thought another piece of the barn roof had pulled loose and hit her. She was afraid to raise her head and give the wind any more to grab, but her legs were numb, and . . .

"I've got you!" a voice shouted from somewhere toward her feet.

"Tyler!" Dana shouted, more grateful than she'd ever been in her life. Now she could feel his arms around her legs and his head pressed against her knees.

But she realized that the wind was still inching her along. She and her cousin would both go over the edge!

"Tyler!" she screamed desperately.

"It's okay. . . . I've . . . hooked my . . . toes . . . into a crack in the rocks!" Tyler yelled into the storm.

Abruptly, Dana's body stopped slipping toward the cliffs.

She and Tyler lay there for a minute or two without saying anything, Dana trying not to choke on the rain pounding into her upturned face.

Finally, she gurgled, "Now what do we do?"

And Tyler's muffled answer came back to her on the wind. "I guess we stay like this till it's over?"

How long is that? Dana asked herself. She tried to remember Hurricane Patricia or Eric, storms she'd experienced herself. Hadn't they lasted eight or ten hours? How long could Tyler hang on to her? How long could his toes stay hooked into the rocks?

Minutes crawled by, while the storm raged around them. Was Tyler's grip loosening? *If only I could sink into these rocks, instead of lying on top of them, practically asking to get blown away!* Dana said to herself.

Then, suddenly, she thought she heard another voice.

No, it's just the wind banging the boards on the stranding barn, she thought. *Nobody would be dumb enough to come out here in a hurricane . . . except me!*

But Dana heard it again. "Lie still—I'm coming for you!"

"It's Hallie!" Tyler's voice rose from around Dana's knees.

But what could Hallie do to help them? All three of them would go over the cliffs!

"We've got a rope!" Hallie yelled.

And Dana's heart skipped a beat.

She didn't hear anything else for what seemed like a long while. Then she felt Tyler moving a little.

"Tyler?!" Dana shrieked, terrified that he was turning her loose.

"I'm tying a rope to his waist!" Hallie yelled to reassure Dana. "Just stay still."

Hallie sounded much closer this time, and soon Dana felt hands reaching up to her own waist. Hallie shoved aside the bottom of Dana's windbreaker, threaded the end of a rope through three of the belt loops in Dana's jeans, and then knotted it.

"Okay!" Hallie shouted. "You and Tyler and I are all hooked to this long rope, and Carter's at the other end, which he knotted to a post outside the barn."

Dana felt good about that, because Carter was a fisherman's kid, and he knew how to tie excellent knots.

"I'll start working my way back toward the barn,

because I'm tied on first," Hallie told her, "and then Tyler next, and when you feel the rope tighten—"

"I'll roll over and crawl after you," Dana said, still gazing upward into the rain, afraid to move anything larger than a finger.

She felt Hallie inching away from her. Dana started counting, just to give herself something else to focus on. When she got to forty-six, Tyler's grip loosened on her legs. He was leaving her, too.

"Tyler . . . I'm slipping!" Dana screamed. Hurricane Fiona was pushing her again, sliding her slowly but steadily toward the cliffs!

"The rope'll stop you!" Carter shouted from the barn.

Sure enough, a few seconds later, the rope tightened on Dana's belt loops. She stopped moving.

"Turn over, Dana!" Hallie called out.

But Dana was frozen, too scared even to raise her head.

"Do it, Dana," Tyler yelled. "We've got you!"

Dana took a deep breath. Then she reached down and grabbed hold of the rope at her waist with both hands. Dana swung her legs sideways, away from the rope— the gusting wind actually helping this time—and then she rolled onto her stomach. Now Dana's head was pointed at the stranding barn, and she was still hanging on to the rope for dear life.

"We're reeling you in," Carter shouted to her.

Dana kept her head down until they'd pulled her all

the way to the edge of the barn, and beyond it. When she finally looked up, she saw three pairs of drenched sneakers right in front of her. But Dana couldn't make herself let the rope go.

"You can stand up now," Hallie said to her.

"Barn blocks a lot of the wind here," Carter added.

"You're okay, Dana," Tyler said, leaning down to pry her fingers away from the rope. "Let go."

Dana started to shiver, and her teeth chattered.

"Nerves," Hallie announced, nodding wisely.

Dana wasn't going to argue with her. Hallie had crawled out on those wet rocks with the rope, after all.

Holding on to the barn siding, Dana pulled herself to her feet. "Thanks, guys," she said to all three of them. "I owe you one—a really big one."

Carter smiled shyly, Hallie shrugged, and Tyler said, "You rescued me on Crab Island—now we're even."

"How did you know we were in trouble?" Dana asked Hallie and Carter.

"We saw part of the barn roof crash into the sliding door," Hallie said. "We thought you might be trapped in the barn. Carter remembered you had some rope in your basement—"

"Saw it when you lent us lights for the festival," Carter explained.

"We tied ourselves together, crawled to the barn, and pulled the shingles away from the door," Hallie went on. "But you weren't in there. Then we spotted you through a window."

"We better get back," Carter told them, "before Tim wakes up."

"He'd dozed off before we left," Hallie said to Dana and Tyler. "If he wakes up, and we're not back safe inside the house, he'll—"

"Yeah, I know—he'll be out here in the storm with his head all banged up, looking for us," Tyler said.

"We might as well stay hooked together," Hallie said. She untied the end of the rope from the post, handed it to Carter, and he knotted it quickly around his own waist.

"Ready?" Carter said to Dana and Tyler.

"Ready." Dana nodded.

The wind didn't seem to be quite as fierce as it had been earlier. With Carter in the lead, the four of them scrambled back across the gravel road and into the kitchen at the lighthouse in record time.

"Sssh," Dana said to Jake, who'd been waiting at the door. He was whining and running in circles around them.

"It's okay—I can hear Tim snoring," Hallie murmured.

As they peeled off their slickers and ponchos, Dana whispered, "Uh . . . guys? I'm not asking anybody to lie or anything, but . . ."

"But you don't see why Tim needs to know about us practically going over the cliff, right?" Tyler continued for her.

"Right," said Dana. "He'd feel awful about it, since he sees himself as the grown-up in charge."

"And there's no real reason to tell Aunt Lissa and Uncle Joe, either, is there?" said Tyler.

He already had a reputation with Dana's mom and dad for not thinking things through first.

"Why worry them? It's over and done with," Dana agreed, "and with any luck, it'll never happen again."

"At least not in exactly the same way," said Hallie. She walked over to the table to check on the kittens in the bread basket. "They're sleeping, too," she whispered. "They are so cute—just like fat little mice!"

"Have you named them?" Tyler asked her.

"Carter says the red one's a boy and the black one's a girl," Hallie replied. "The girl's name is Fiona—"

Dana, Tyler, and Carter nodded—a perfect name, considering.

"And I'm going to call the boy Carter," Hallie said. "It was Carter who really saved the day."

Carter turned bright red. But Dana thought he looked pleased.

CHAPTER TEN

Back inside the lighthouse after the close call near the cliffs, Tyler looked up at the kitchen clock. It was barely two in the afternoon, and enough stuff had happened already to fill several days, if not a whole week!

They checked on Tim in the living room. "One heck of a headache," he said drowsily and went back to sleep.

Then Tyler, Dana, Hallie, and Carter changed out of their wet clothes. Dana lent Hallie jeans and a polo shirt, and Tyler found khakis and a T-shirt for Carter. They went into the kitchen again and made cheese sandwiches while they listened to SHOR-FM.

". . . much of the damage in Rockport so far is the result of major flooding in the downtown area—tides are running six to eight feet above normal," the announcer said. "Thousands of area residents are without electricity or phone service. Some of the roads leading into town have been washed out, including Harbor Lane. . . ."

Tyler, Dana, Hallie, and Carter glanced at one another.

"I guess we're going to be here for a while," Hallie said to Carter.

". . . and all flights have been canceled at the Wilton airport," the announcer went on.

"I'll bet Mom and Dad are flipping out in California!" Dana said.

"The eye of the storm has passed directly over Indian Beach," the announcer went on. "Fiona's making her way inland, losing strength as she goes. The National Weather Service expects her to be downgraded to a tropical storm by this evening. . . ."

"So the wind really is dying down," Dana said.

The four of them walked over to a kitchen window and peered out at the water-logged Point.

"I think the rain's letting up a little, too," Tyler said, adding, "we survived Fiona!"

"You sound like a T-shirt," Hallie told him, laughing.

She and Dana turned away to tend to the kittens, who were meowing from their nest in the basket. But Carter didn't leave the window. Even though there wasn't much to see, he gazed into the distance with an uneasy look on his face.

Carter must be really worried about his dad, out there somewhere on the Bonnie Jean, *Tyler said to himself. And maybe about Charlie and Grandpa Mote, too—that old house could have blown apart by now!*

"Hey, do you want to go up in the tower?" Tyler said to Carter. "Get a better view?"

"Sure!" Carter said eagerly.

"We'll come, too," Dana said.

The group tiptoed through the living room—Tim was dozing under his blanket, with Jake snoring right beside him—and across the dining room to the low door in the far wall. The iron steps of the tower were steep, and they curved around and around like a corkscrew, narrowing as the thick stone walls of the tower narrowed.

First Tyler, then Carter and Hallie, reached the top of the lighthouse. Dana stopped on the last step, because only three kids would fit on the tiny metal platform with its 360-degree view. When they stared through the thick glass panels at the rainy Atlantic, they gasped. Towering gray-blue waves stretched to the horizon, so high that they completely hid Gull, Pelham, and Perth islands, where harbor seals hauled out, and thousands of seabirds nested.

"The waves were huge for two or three days after Hurricane Eric," Dana remembered.

How could anybody maneuver a boat through those seas without being swamped? Tyler wondered. *Even the best sailors and fishermen?*

He glanced at Carter, who looked almost sick with worry.

How would I feel if it were my dad out there? Tyler said to himself. *And why did I suggest we climb the tower? I must have been crazy—now Carter feels even worse!*

Then Hallie said, "It's too stormy to see all the way to Rockport, but Crab Island's still standing." She was facing toward Badger Bay and the mainland. Crab Island was a low jumble of rocks strung across the entrance to the bay. Hallie went on, "Wow, Harbor Lane's totally flooded, and—"

"I see somebody out walking!" Dana exclaimed. "No, *two* people!"

"Out in this storm? You're kidding!" said Tyler, turning around to face Harbor Lane. Or at least where Harbor Lane should have been. Now it was more like Harbor *Lake*.

But Dana was right. Two people were making their way across higher ground on the far side of the road, ponchos flapping in the wind.

They were still too far away for Tyler to recognize. It only took Carter a glimpse, though. "That's Charlie and Grandpa!" he exclaimed.

Carter squeezed around Dana and headed down the lighthouse stairs, Hallie following him. Before Tyler could start after them, Dana said, "Tyler, what's that in the dolphin pool?"

The bird's-eye view from the platform at the top of the tower let them see straight into it.

"More boards got ripped off the shed roof," Tyler said. "Do you think Bonnie and Claude are okay?"

Dana was already on her way downstairs to find out.

She and Tyler grabbed their rain gear off the hooks in the kitchen and stepped outside again, closing the door on Jake.

The weather *was* changing. The wind wasn't half as strong as it had been, and the rain was more of a heavy drizzle than a downpour. Carter and Hallie were splashing down the gravel road to meet Charlie and Grandpa Mote who had almost reached the mailboxes.

Tyler and Dana hurried over to the dolphin pool instead. At the near end of it, another heavy section of shed roof lay half in and half out of the water, its edges jagged and studded with nails.

The two whales were swimming around at the far end of the pool.

"I guess they're okay," Dana said. "At least . . ." Then she stopped herself.

Claude was having trouble maneuvering. Instead of performing with his usual underwater daring, Claude was swimming slowly, and his turns were stiff and awkward. When Tyler bent down for a closer look at the young pilot whale, he spotted a reddish-brown stain in the water that seemed to follow Claude around.

"Dana, I think Claude's bleeding," Tyler said.

"It's coming from his left side. And maybe his pectoral fin," Dana agreed uneasily, edging around the pool toward the whales. "It *is* his fin, Tyler," she called out in a moment. "It's torn near the tip—the tip's just sort of hanging there."

Tyler knew that Claude would never be able to swim properly with a torn fin. Which would mean that he could never be released into the Atlantic. The fin had to be sewn back together, and the sooner the better.

"What can *we* do?" Dana was saying forlornly. "There aren't any Neptuners for miles except Tim, and Tim's in no shape to deal with a wounded whale."

But then Tyler told himself, *Hey, we're Neptuners, too!* And he thought of all the things he'd seen and learned at the Point over the last six months.

"Remember how Bonnie and Claude wouldn't eat when they first got here . . . ," he began.

"And the Neptuners drained most of the water out of the pool, so they could stuff food down the whales' throats without having them thrash around and hurt themselves or someone else," Dana went on, nodding.

"We could do the same thing and work on Claude's fin," Tyler said.

"Bandaging won't do any good—it should be sewn," Dana said. "Who's going to do that? Could you sew Claude up?"

"I could try," Tyler said. He'd watched Dr. Bucalo wield a needle and thread quite a few times. "But I'll bet Grandpa Mote could do it better."

"He knows how to sew whales?" Dana said in disbelief.

"No, how to sew *sails*," said Tyler. "And whale skin can't be any harder to sew than really heavy canvas."

"Do you think he'd be willing to do it for us?" said

Dana doubtfully. She probably had the twins' dad in mind, with his disapproving opinions about Project Neptune.

"We can ask him," Tyler said, pointing down the gravel road. "Here they come!"

CHAPTER ELEVEN

The twins' granddad *must* have been tired.

He and Charlie had ridden in the old truck for as far as they could up Harbor Lane, until it died in the storm. Then they'd walked, and even dog-paddled, the rest of the way to Parsons Point through the tail end of Hurricane Fiona. Plus Grandpa Mote didn't just look old—he looked *ancient* to Dana, with his long white beard and crinkled, leathery skin.

But as soon as Tyler and Dana explained about Claude, he was ready to try.

"Never been this close to a live pilot whale," he said, peering down at Bonnie and Claude in the dolphin pool. "In the old days, people used to smoke 'em and eat 'em. They'd drive one or two ashore, and the whole rest of the pod would follow those in, and there'd be forty or fifty of 'em floundering on Indian Beach. . . ." He must have noticed Dana's horrified expression, because he stopped himself, shifted gears, and added,

"I've sewed up my own cats and dogs—whales can't be so all-fired different. But how do we go about it? Can't do it underwater—not that good a swimmer."

"We'll pump most of the water out of the pool," Tyler explained to him, "so the whales can't swim away from us."

First the six of them dragged the heavy, jagged section of shed roof out of the water. Then they carried Neptune's gasoline-powered pump out of the stranding barn and set it up next to the pool. Tyler screwed a length of hose into one side of the pump to suck the water up, and another hose into the other side to carry the water away. While Charlie and Carter and their granddad got the pump going, Dana, Tyler, and Hallie found surgical needles and thread in the cabinet in Dr. Bucalo's examining room.

Carter and Grandpa Mote headed for the lighthouse to check on Tim. "Just don't tell him about the whale," Dana warned them.

Then she, Tyler, Hallie, and Charlie kept an eye on Bonnie and Claude and waited in the rain for the pump to do its business.

"When you guys didn't come back this morning, Grandpa and I went out looking for you," Charlie told Tyler and Dana. "We'd barely made it to the end of Roanoke when we ran into Mr. Haner, and he told us he'd seen you on Harbor Lane."

"*Who* is Mr. Haner?" Hallie asked him.

"A card-playing friend of Grandpa's—he knows Carter and me," Charlie replied. "He was working on his car on the road."

"Oh, right," said Tyler.

"The bossy guy under the hood," said Hallie.

"Carter didn't say he knew him," Dana said.

"Carter doesn't say much," Charlie answered, shrugging. "Anyway, it wasn't hard for us to figure out you were heading for the Point to look for Jake. It just took us a while to get here."

He smiled at them, but behind the smile he looked really uneasy. Dana wondered if Charlie had heard anything about his dad or any of the other Rockport fishermen, riding out the storm at sea.

Then Grandpa Mote and Carter came back from the lighthouse with good news. "Tim's okay," Carter announced.

"You can always tell by looking into the eyes if there's something to worry about," Grandpa Mote told them. "And Tim's eyes look fine. He'll probably have a mean headache for a few days, but that's about all. Now"—he gazed down at the pilot whales himself—"got my sewing kit?"

The group waited until the water drained down to about a foot in depth, and Bonnie and Claude were basically beached on their stomachs at the bottom. Then, one at a time, all six humans slipped down into the pool.

Bonnie was skittish. She scooted away from them, using her dorsal fins to push herself along. Claude lay quietly, gazing at them curiously as they waded slowly toward him.

"Hallie and I'll stand on the far side to try to keep him from moving away," Tyler whispered, skirting Claude's large flukes. "Carter and Charlie can stand on the near side. And Dana—you help Mr. Mote."

"And if Claude starts thrashing, jump out of the way. He could break your leg with his tail," Dana added.

Whales tended to be gentle creatures and maybe Claude somehow understood that the group of humans was trying to help him. Or maybe he was able to recognize Dana and Tyler's scents, the way Ellie the blind seal did, and felt more comfortable about having his space invaded. Whatever the reason, Claude hardly even twitched when Dana and Grandpa Mote squatted down next to his wounded left dorsal fin. He exhaled through his blowhole with a loud *whooosh*. When he breathed in again, it sounded like a sigh.

"It's not a clean slice—it's torn ragged," Grandpa Mote whispered to Dana after he'd taken a close look at the wound.

Dana nodded, remembering the jagged edge of the section of roof that had landed in the pool, and the rusty nails that had been sticking out of it.

"I'll do my best," Grandpa Mote murmured, squaring his shoulders.

Dana grasped the top of Claude's fin with both hands, trying to hold it steady, while the twins' granddad started stitching up the wound near the bottom. He'd poke the needle quickly through the whale's thick skin, pull it out on the back side and bring the thread through the hole, and let Claude wiggle his fin a bit. Then Grandpa Mote would push the needle through from the back side, and tighten the thread again and knot the stitch.

It made Dana feel sort of queasy to watch—the edges of Claude's wound looked too much like raw steak, up so close. But she wanted to make sure Mr. Mote didn't miss a stitch.

And it was slow going. But Claude was a great patient. His pal, Bonnie, seemed more concerned about what the humans were up to than he was. She would edge closer to them on her own dorsal fins. Then she'd push herself away, scolding them with loud clicking sounds.

Finally, Grandpa Mote whispered to Dana, "That'll do it. It's not neat, but it'll hold."

He cut the remaining thread off with a pocketknife and stood up, backing away from the pilot whale. Dana released the top of Claude's fin and stepped back herself. Tyler, Hallie, Charlie, and Carter moved away from the whale, too.

Silently, they climbed out of the pool.

Then Dana and Tyler gave each other high fives. "We did it!" Dana exclaimed.

They gave more high fives to Hallie and the twins, and the twins high-fived their granddad.

"Thank you so much, Mr. Mote," Dana said to him.

"Nothing to it. Just like my own animals. Except bigger, of course," said Grandpa Mote.

"I have a good slogan for a T-shirt," Hallie said. " 'Project Neptune, the Next Generation!' "

"And it's stopped raining," Tyler said.

They could even see the sun peeking out from under a dark-gray cloud bank.

Right about then, Jane Hodges's yellow Land Rover turned into the gravel road. She'd been a Neptuner since Dana was a little kid. Sue Larkin, another volunteer, was sitting in the passenger seat.

"Did you make it okay?" Jane yelled through the window. "Your phone's still out. Did the stranding barn hold up all right? And all of the animals?"

"We finally got through to Dr. Bucalo!" Sue was calling from her side. "And Walter McGrath. They're on their way, even if they have to walk. And we have a customer for Project Neptune in the back."

Dana and Tyler and the other kids ran to the truck as it groaned to a stop. On a towel behind the front seat, a baby seal lay on its side, so covered with sand that they couldn't even tell what kind it was. It was barely breathing.

Another truck and car were bouncing up the road toward the stranding barn. Project Neptune was already back in business.

CHAPTER TWELVE

"Got anything to eat in the lighthouse?" Charlie said to Dana and Tyler then.

"Cheese sandwiches okay?" said Dana.

"I could eat about a dozen of 'em," Carter replied.

As the group walked toward the house, Dana heard Charlie asking his granddad, "Could we try the Coast Guard station again?"

"As soon as we get inside," Grandpa Mote replied.

"Our phone's not working," Dana said to them apologetically.

"Grandpa has a cell phone," Carter murmured.

Dana stared at the little old man with the wispy white beard. Grandpa Mote was full of surprises!

As soon as he'd peeled off his slicker in the Chapins' kitchen, the twins' granddad reached into a side pocket of his overalls. He pulled a cell phone out of a plastic bag, punched in a number, and put the receiver to his ear.

"We couldn't get through to them before we left town," Charlie said as he, Carter, Dana, Tyler, and Hallie watched Grandpa Mote's face. "Maybe all the lines are down, or—"

"It's ringing," Grandpa Mote said suddenly. "Which doesn't necessarily mean that it's—Hello? . . . Hello! Is this Rockport Coast Guard? . . . This is Zeke Mote. . . . Right. Have you heard anything from the *Bonnie Jean?* That's my son's boat. . . .Yes . . . yes!" Old Mr. Mote's brown, wrinkled face creased into a wide smile. "So he's okay—"

Charlie and Carter beamed with relief.

"And the Novaks and the Millers are, too?" their granddad went on. The Novaks and Millers were more Rockport fishermen.

"Nope, that'll do it, thanks," Grandpa Mote said into the cell phone, ready to disconnect. When Dana waved at him frantically, though, he added, "Hold on a minute—"

"Is there some way they can get in touch with the Meyerses at WLIR," Dana said hurriedly, "to let them know we're at the lighthouse with Jake, and we're safe?"

"And my aunt Gretchen?" said Hallie. "She's probably fit to be tied by now!"

Luckily, both WLIR and the FM station in Rockport had short-wave radios like the Coast Guard's. Dana, Tyler, Jake, Hallie, and the twins and their granddad were sitting in the kitchen, eating sandwiches, pickles, and chips, when they heard the announcements go out over SHOR-FM. "The Chapin kids and Jake and Hallie Wade want everyone to know that they rode out this storm just fine at the Parsons Point lighthouse. More updates: A hundred-fifty-year-old maple tree smashed through the roof of the Rockport Middle School, and I'm afraid opening day of the fall semester will have to be postponed until repairs can be made—"

"Yay!" Charlie and Carter cheered. They were not all that crazy about starting school in a week.

And Grandpa Mote said, "It's an ill wind that blows no one any good," before taking a bite of pickle.

"Sssh!" Hallie shushed them all. "Listen."

"Ten-foot waves are still pounding Indian Beach, taking a large part of the sand away," the announcer continued.

"The throbbing's slacking off in my big toe," Grandpa Mote reported then, holding up his left foot in its damp sock. "The storm's just about gone."

"Yeah, all that's left is the cleanup!" Tim called out from his bed on the living-room floor.

And Dana had a feeling *that* was going to be quite a job.

The back door of the house swung open and Walter McGrath with Lou Green and Donny Nolan, two other Neptuners, stepped inside.

"Tim okay?" Lou asked the group at the table, crossing the kitchen to see for himself.

Donny said, "Maybe we'd better start making sandwiches. We'll all be here for a while."

"We could definitely use some help in the stranding barn," Walter told them. "Two more young seals were just brought in and a small bottlenose and . . ."

"I'll go," said Hallie, standing up.

"Us, too," said Charlie.

"I've thought of the best T-shirt yet," Tyler said to Dana as they all hurried out the door. "Project Neptune—"

"Rules!" Dana finished for him.

AFTERWORD

Atlantic coast hurricanes, like the one in this story, form in the tropics. Warm, moist air rises from the ocean there, and is set spinning counterclockwise by the rotation of the earth. As the air continues to rise, it cools, releasing moisture in the form of thunderstorms, then drops back to the surface of the ocean, where it is warmed and pulled up again.

The storm system becomes more organized, with winds and strong thunderstorms rotating around a calm, central "eye." When the spinning winds have increased to thirty-nine miles an hour, the system is upgraded to a tropical storm and given a name. And if the winds grow stronger than seventy-four miles an hour, the storm achieves hurricane status.

Often more than three hundred miles across, a hurricane is ranked according to the speed of its rotating winds. A Category 1 hurricane has winds registering less than 95 miles an hour, and it will cause only minor damage. The winds of a Category 5 hurricane, however, will register over 155 miles per hour, so powerful that small buildings may be overturned, or even blown away. A Category 5 storm is strong enough to push ashore an eighteen-foot storm surge.

For centuries people tried to read the weather themselves. During hurricane season, from June 1 through November, they'd look for hazy, red sunsets, hot, sticky air, and growing swells on the ocean. And if their barometers rose and then dropped suddenly, a hurricane might be on its way.

But sometimes the warning signs weren't so apparent.

At the end of September in 1938, Long Island, New York, and the coasts of Connecticut, Rhode Island, and Massachusetts were hit by an unexpected and devastating storm. Most Atlantic hurricanes lose their strength as they move into the colder waters of New England. But the hurricane of '38 ripped houses apart with its winds and sent a ten-foot storm surge several miles inland. In the town where I live now, on the East End of Long Island, the surge swamped Main Street with six feet of water, and many people drowned.

Hundreds of millions of dollars of damage was done to homes and property in the area. Seven hundred people died before the storm finally broke up in New Hampshire.

These days, Hurricane Hunters from the U.S. Air Force Reserve fly through storms to measure wind speed and direction, helping to predict where a hurricane will go. Meteorologists get even more information from sophisticated weather satellites and radar, tracking a potentially dangerous storm from the moment of its birth in the tropics. They follow its path toward the coastline, and chart fairly accurately where it's likely to make landfall. They can warn people in time for them to evacuate safely, since the forward motion of a hurricane is usually not much faster than fifteen or twenty miles per hour.

Successful evacuations have cut the number of hurricane-related deaths to a fraction of what they might have been without early warnings. But the huge storms continue to cause tremendous damage. Five hundred thousand people were evacuated before Hurricane Andrew made landfall in south Florida in September, 1992, and only 23 people died as a direct result of the storm. But 160,000 were left homeless, and 300,000 jobs were affected. Almost 80,000 people left the area and never returned.

For an up-to-date, weather-satellite image of the Atlantic region, visit:

http://www.ns.doe.ca/weather/hurricane/sat.html

For an illustration of the formation of a hurricane, visit:

http://www.windows.umich.edu/earth/images/ hurricane_formation_jpg_image.html

For an example of a hurricane tracking chart, visit:

http://www.yatcom.com/neworl/weather/track_ch.gif

For a satellite photograph of Hurricane Andrew, showing its well-defined eye, visit:

**http://www.windows.umich.edu/earth/images/
hurricane_andrw_image.html**

For photographs taken before and after a storm surge that struck the coast of South Carolina in 1989, visit:

**http://www.windows.umich.edu/earth/Atmosphere/
hurricane/surge_inset.html**

And for the Home Page of the Hurricane Hunters, visit:

http://www.hurricanehunters.com

Join in All the Daring Environmental Adventure with

NEPTUNE ADVENTURES
by Susan Saunders

Parsons Point lighthouse on the Atlantic coast, home to cousins Dana and Tyler Chapin, is part of Project Neptune, a nonprofit operation that works with sick and injured sea animals.

DANGER ON CRAB ISLAND
79488-8/$3.99 US/$4.99 Can

Tyler's daring escapade to explore Crab Island has him trapped in deadly currents...and only Dana knows he's out there.

DISASTER AT PARSONS POINT
79489-6/$3.99 US/$4.99 Can

There's a huge oil spill in the Atlantic that threatens the life of the sea animals and the local fishing industry.

THE DOLPHIN TRAP
79490-X/$3.99 US/$4.99 Can

Tyler's really upset when he learns that Boone, a bottlenose dolphin trained by the Navy, has been turned over to Project Neptune—to be held in captivity.

Buy these books at your local bookstore or use this coupon for ordering:

Mail to: Avon Books, Dept BP, Box 767, Rte 2, Dresden, TN 38225   G
Please send me the book(s) I have checked above.
❏ My check or money order—no cash or CODs please—for $_____is enclosed (please add $1.50 per order to cover postage and handling—Canadian residents add 7% GST). U.S. residents make checks payable to Avon Books; Canada residents make checks payable to Hearst Book Group of Canada.
❏ Charge my VISA/MC Acct#_____Exp Date_____
Minimum credit card order is two books or $7.50 (please add postage and handling charge of $1.50 per order—Canadian residents add 7% GST). For faster service, call 1-800-762-0779. Prices and numbers are subject to change without notice. Please allow six to

Name_____
Address_____
City_____State/Zip_____
Telephone No._____   NA 0698